THE GREAT RETURN

THE GREAT RETURN
By ARTHUR MACHEN

Angelico Press

For information, address:
Angelico Press, Ltd.
169 Monitor St.
Brooklyn, NY 11222
www.angelicopress.com

paper 978-1-62138-772-5
cloth 978-1-62138-773-2

Cover design
by Michael Schrauzer

To

D. P. M.

CONTENTS

THE
GREAT RETURN

CHAPTER I

THE RUMOUR OF THE MARVELLOUS

THERE are strange things lost and forgotten in obscure corners of the newspaper. I often think that the most extraordinary item of intelligence that I have read in print appeared a few years ago in the London Press. It came from a well-known and most respected news agency; I imagine it was in all the papers. It was astounding.

The circumstances necessary—not to the understanding of this paragraph, for that is out of the question—but, we will say, to the understanding of the events which made it possible, are these. We had invaded Thibet, and there had been trouble in the hierarchy of that country, and a personage known as the Tashai Lama had taken refuge with us in India. He went on pilgrimage from one Buddhist shrine to another, and came at last to a holy mountain of Buddhism, the name of which I have forgotten. And thus the morning paper:

His Holiness the Tashai Lama then ascended the Mountain and was transfigured.—Reuter.

That was all. And from that day to this I have never heard a word of explanation or comment on this amazing statement.

.   .   .   .   .

There was no more, it seemed, to be said. "Reuter," apparently, thought he had made his simple statement of the facts of the case, had thereby done his duty, and so it all ended. Nobody, so far as I know, ever wrote to any paper asking what Reuter meant by it, or what the Tashai Lama meant by it. I suppose the fact was that nobody cared twopence about the matter ; and so this strange event—if there were any such event—was exhibited to us for a moment, and the lantern show revolved to other spectacles.

This is an extreme instance of the manner in which the marvellous is flashed out to us and then withdrawn behind its black veils and concealments ; but I have known of other cases. Now and again, at intervals of a few years, there appear in the newspapers strange stories of the strange doings of what are technically called *poltergeists*. Some house, often a lonely farm, is suddenly subjected to an infernal bombardment. Great stones crash through the windows, thunder down the chimneys, impelled by no visible hand. The plates and cups and saucers are whirled from the dresser into the middle of the kitchen, no one can say how or by what agency. Upstairs the big bedstead and an old chest or two are heard bounding on the floor as if in a mad ballet. Now and then such doings as these excite a whole neighbourhood ; sometimes a London paper sends a man down to make an investigation. He writes half a column of description on the Monday, a couple of paragraphs on the Tuesday, and then returns to town. Nothing has been explained, the matter vanishes away ; and nobody cares. The tale trickles for a day or two through the Press, and then instantly disappears, like an Australian stream, into the bowels of darkness. It is possible, I suppose, that this singular incuriousness as to marvellous events and reports is not wholly unaccountable. It may be that the events in question are, as it were, psychic accidents and misadventures. They are not meant to happen, or, rather, to be manifested. They belong to the world on the other side of the dark curtain ; and it is only by some queer mischance that a corner of that curtain is twitched aside for an instant. Then—for an instant—we see ; but the personages whom Mr. Kipling calls the Lords of Life and Death take care that we do not see too much. Our business is with things higher and things lower, with things different, anyhow ; and on the whole we are not suffered to distract ourselves with that which does not really concern us. The Transfiguration of the Lama and the tricks of the *poltergeist* are evidently no affairs of ours ; we raise an uninterested eyebrow and pass on—to poetry or to statistics.

    .   .   .   .   .

Be it noted ; I am not professing any fervent personal belief in the reports to which I have alluded. For all I know, the Lama, in spite of Reuter, was not transfigured, and the *poltergeist*, in spite of the late Mr. Andrew Lang, may in reality be only mischievous Polly, the servant girl at the farm. And to go farther: I do not know that I should be justified in putting either of these cases of the marvellous in line with a chance paragraph that caught my eye last summer ; for this had not, on the face of it at all events, anything wildly out of the common. Indeed, I dare say that I should not have read it, should not have seen it, if it had not contained the name of a place which I had once visited, which had then moved me in an odd manner that I could not understand. Indeed, I am sure that this particular paragraph deserves to stand alone, for even if the *poltergeist* be a real *poltergeist*, it merely reveals the psychic whimsicality of some region that is not our region. There were better things and more relevant things behind the few lines dealing with Llantrisant, the little town by the sea in Arfonshire.

Not on the surface, I must say, for the cutting—I have preserved it—reads as follows :—

LLANTRISANT.—The season promises very favourably : temperature of the sea yesterday at noon, 65 deg. Remarkable occurrences are supposed to have taken place during the recent Revival. The lights have not been observed lately. "The Crown." "The Fisherman's Rest."

The style was odd certainly; knowing a little of newspapers, I could see that the figure called, I think, *tmesis*, or cutting, had been generously employed; the exuberances of the local correspondent had been pruned by a Fleet Street expert. And these poor men are often hurried; but what did those "lights" mean? What strange matters had the vehement blue pencil blotted out and brought to naught?

That was my first thought, and then, thinking still of Llantrisant and how I had first discovered it and found it strange, I read the paragraph again, and was saddened almost to see, as I thought, the obvious explanation. I had forgotten for the moment that it was war-time, that scares and rumours and terrors about traitorous signals and flashing lights were current everywhere by land and sea; someone, no doubt, had been watching innocent farmhouse windows and thoughtless fanlights of lodging-houses;

these were the "lights" that had not been observed lately.

I found out afterwards that the Llantrisant correspondent had no such treasonous lights in his mind, but something very different. Still; what do we know? He may have been mistaken, "the great rose of fire" that came over the deep may have been the port light of a coasting-ship. Did it shine at last from the old chapel on the headland? Possibly; or possibly it was the doctor's lamp at Sarnau, some miles away. I have had wonderful opportunities lately of analysing the marvels of lying, conscious and unconscious; and indeed almost incredible feats in this way can be performed. If I incline to the less likely explanation of the "lights" at Llantrisant, it is merely because this explanation seems to me to be altogether congruous with the "remarkable occurrences" of the newspaper paragraph.

After all, if rumour and gossip and hearsay are crazy things to be utterly neglected and laid aside: on the other hand, evidence is evidence, and when a couple of reputable surgeons assert, as they do assert in the case of Olwen Phillips, Croeswen, Llantrisant, that there has been a "kind of resurrection of the body," it is merely foolish to say that these things don't happen. The girl was a mass of tuberculosis, she was within a few hours of death; she is now full of life. And so, I do not believe that the rose of fire was merely a ship's light, magnified and transformed by dreaming Welsh sailors.

.   .   .   .   .

But now I am going forward too fast. I have not dated the paragraph, so I cannot give the exact day of its appearance, but I think it was somewhere between the second and third week of June. I cut it out partly because it was about Llantrisant, partly because of the " remarkable occurrences." I have an appetite for these matters, though I also have this misfortune, that I require evidence before I am ready to credit them, and I have a sort of lingering hope that some day I shall be able to elaborate some scheme or theory of such things.

But in the meantime, as a temporary measure, I hold what I call the doctrine of the jig-saw puzzle. That is: this remarkable occurrence, and that, and the other may be, and usually are, of no significance. Coincidence and chance and unsearchable causes will now and again make clouds that are undeniable fiery dragons, and potatoes that resemble Eminent Statesmen exactly and minutely in every feature, and rocks that are like eagles and lions. All this is nothing; it is when you get your set of odd shapes and find that they fit into one another, and at last that they are but parts of a large design; it is then that research grows interesting and indeed amazing, it is then that one queer form confirms the other, that the whole plan displayed justifies, corroborates, explains each separate piece.

So; it was within a week or ten days after I had read the paragraph about Llantrisant and had cut it out that I got a letter from a friend who was taking an early holiday in those regions.

"You will be interested," he wrote, "to hear that they have taken to ritualistic practices at Llantrisant. I went into the church the other day, and instead of smelling like a damp vault as usual, it was positively reeking with incense."

I knew better than that. The old parson was a firm Evangelical; he would rather have burnt sulphur in his church than incense any day. So I could not make out this report at all; and went down to Arfon a few weeks later determined to investigate this and any other remarkable occurrence at Llantrisant.

CHAPTER II

ODOURS OF PARADISE

I WENT down to Arfon in the very heat and bloom and fragrance of the wonderful summer that they were enjoying there. In London there was no such weather; it rather seemed as if the horror and fury of the war had mounted to the very skies and were there reigning. In the mornings the sun burnt down upon the city with a heat that scorched and consumed; but then clouds heavy and horrible would roll together from all quarters of the heavens, and early in the afternoon the air would darken, and a storm of thunder and lightning, and furious, hissing rain would fall upon the streets. Indeed, the torment of the world was in the London weather. The city wore a terrible vesture; within our hearts was dread; without we were clothed in black clouds and angry fire.

It is certain that I cannot show in any words the utter peace of that Welsh coast to which I came ; one sees, I think, in such a change a figure of the passage from the disquiets and the fears of earth to the peace of paradise. A land that seemed to be in a holy, happy dream, a sea that changed all the while from olivine to emerald, from emerald to sapphire, from sapphire to amethyst, that washed in white foam at the bases of the firm, grey rocks, and about the huge crimson bastions that hid the western bays and inlets of the waters ; to this land I came, and to hollows that were purple and odorous with wild thyme, wonderful with many tiny, exquisite flowers. There was benediction in centaury, pardon in eye-bright, joy in lady's slipper ; and so the weary eyes were refreshed, looking now at the little flowers and the happy bees about them, now on the magic mirror of the deep, changing from marvel to marvel with the passing of the great white clouds, with the brightening of the sun. And the ears, torn with jangle and racket and idle, empty noise, were soothed and comforted by the ineffable, unutterable, unceasing murmur, as the tides swam to and fro, uttering mighty, hollow voices in the caverns of the rocks.

·   ·   ·   ·   ·

For three or four days I rested in the sun and smelt the savour of the blossoms and of the salt water, and then, refreshed, I remembered that there was something queer about Llantrisant that I might as well investigate. It was no great thing that I thought to find, for, it will be remembered, I had ruled out the apparent oddity of the reporter's—or commissioner's?—reference to lights, on the ground that he must have been referring to some local panic about signalling to the enemy; who had certainly torpedoed a ship or two off Lundy in the Bristol Channel. All that I had to go upon was the reference to the " remarkable occurrences " at some revival, and then that letter of Jackson's, which spoke of Llantrisant church as " reeking " with incense, a wholly incredible and impossible state of things. Why, old Mr. Evans, the rector, looked upon coloured stoles as the very robe of Satan and his angels, as things dear to the heart of the Pope of Rome. But as to incense ! As I have already familiarly observed, I knew better.

But as a hard matter of fact, this may be worth noting : when I went over to Llantrisant on Monday, August 9th, I visited the church, and it was still fragrant and exquisite with the odour of rare gums that had fumed there.

. . . . .

Now I happened to have a slight acquaintance with the rector. He was a most courteous and delightful old man, and on my last visit he had come across me in the churchyard, as I was admiring the very fine Celtic cross that stands there. Besides the beauty of the interlaced ornament there is an inscription in Ogham on one of the edges, concerning which the learned dispute; it is altogether one of the more famous crosses of Celtdom. Mr. Evans, I say, seeing me looking at the cross, came up and began to give me, the stranger, a résumé—somewhat of a shaky and uncertain résumé, I found afterwards—of the various debates and questions that had arisen as to the exact meaning of the inscription, and I was amused to detect an evident but underlying belief of his own : that the supposed Ogham characters were, in fact, due to boys' mischief and weather and the passing of the ages. But then I happened to put a question as to the sort of stone of which the cross was made, and the rector brightened amazingly. He began to talk geology, and, I think, demonstrated that the cross or the material for it must have been brought to Llantrisant from the south-west coast of Ireland. This struck me as interesting, because it was curious evidence of the migrations of the Celtic saints, whom the rector, I was delighted to find, looked upon as good Protestants, though shaky on the subject of crosses; and so, with concessions on my part, we got on very well. Thus, with all this to the good, I was emboldened to call upon him.

I found him altered. Not that he was aged; indeed, he was rather made young, with a singular brightening upon his face, and something of joy upon it that I had not seen before, that I have seen on very few faces of men. We talked of the war, of course, since that is not to be avoided; of the farming prospects of the county; of general things, till I ventured to remark that I had been in the church, and had been surprised to find it perfumed with incense.

" You have made some alterations in the service since I was here last? You use incense now? "

The old man looked at me strangely, and hesitated.

"No," he said, "there has been no change. I use no incense in the church. I should not venture to do so."

"But," I was beginning, "the whole church is as if High Mass had just been sung there, and——"

He cut me short, and there was a certain grave solemnity in his manner that struck me almost with awe.

"I know you are a railer," he said, and the phrase coming from this mild old gentleman astonished me unutterably. "You are a railer and a bitter railer; I have read articles that you have written, and I know your contempt and your hatred for those you call Protestants in your derision; though your grandfather, the vicar of Caerleon-on-Usk, called himself Protestant and was proud of it, and your great-grand-uncle Hezekiah, *ffeiriad coch yr Castletown*—the Red Priest of Castletown—was a great man with the Methodists in his day, and the people flocked by their thousands when he administered the Sacrament. I was born and brought up in Glamorganshire, and old men have wept as they told me of the weeping and contrition that there was when the Red Priest broke the Bread and raised the Cup. But you are a railer, and see nothing but the outside and the show. You are not worthy of this mystery that has been done here."

I went out from his presence rebuked indeed, and justly rebuked; but rather amazed. It is curiously true that the Welsh are still one people, one family almost, in a manner that the English cannot understand, but I had never thought that this old clergyman would have known anything of my ancestry or their doings. And as for my articles and such-like, I knew that the country clergy sometimes read, but I had fancied my pronouncements sufficiently obscure, even in London, much more in Arfon.

But so it happened, and so I had no explanation from the rector of Llantrisant of the strange circumstance, that his church was full of incense and odours of paradise.

. . . . .

I went up and down the ways of Llantrisant wondering, and came to the harbour, which is a little place, with little quays where some small coasting trade still lingers.

A brigantine was at anchor here, and very lazily in the sunshine they were loading it with anthracite ; for it is one of the oddities of Llantrisant that there is a small colliery in the heart of the wood on the hillside. I crossed a causeway which parts the outer harbour from the inner harbour, and settled down on a rocky beach hidden under a leafy hill. The tide was going out, and some children were playing on the wet sand, while two ladies—their mothers, I suppose—talked together as they sat comfortably on their rugs at a little distance from me.

At first they talked of the war, and I made myself deaf, for of that talk one gets enough, and more than enough, in London. Then there was a period of silence, and the conversation had passed to quite a different topic when I caught the thread of it again. I was sitting on the further side of a big rock, and I do not think that the two ladies had noticed my approach. However, though they spoke of strange things, they spoke of nothing which made it necessary for me to announce my presence.

" And, after all," one of them was saying, " what is it all about ? I can't make out what is come to the people."

This speaker was a Welshwoman ; I recognised the clear, over-emphasised consonants, and a faint suggestion of an accent. Her friend came from the Midlands, and it turned out that they had only known each other for a few days. Theirs was a friendship of the beach and of bathing ; such friendships are common at small seaside places.

" There is certainly something odd about the people here. I have never been to Llantrisant before, you know ; indeed, this is the first time we've been in Wales for our holidays, and knowing nothing about the ways of the people and not being accustomed to hear Welsh spoken, I thought, perhaps, it must be my imagination. But you think there really is something a little queer ? "

" I can tell you this : that I have been in two minds whether I should not write to my husband and ask him to take me and the children away. You know where I am at Mrs. Morgan's, and the Morgans' sitting-room is just the other side of the passage, and sometimes they leave the door open, so that I can hear what they say quite plainly. And you see I understand the Welsh, though they don't know it. And I hear them saying the most alarming things ! "

" What sort of things ? "

" Well, indeed, it sounds like some kind of a religious service, but it's not Church of England, I know that. Old Morgan begins it, and the wife and children answer. Something like : ' Blessed be God for the messengers of Paradise.' ' Blessed be His Name for Paradise in the meat and in the drink.' ' Thanksgiving for the old offering.' ' Thanksgiving for the appearance of the old altar.' ' Praise for the joy of the ancient garden.' ' Praise for the return of those that have been long absent.' And all that sort of thing. It is nothing but madness."

" Depend upon it," said the lady from the Midlands, " there's no real harm in it. They're Dissenters ; some new sect, I dare say. You know some Dissenters are very queer in their ways."

" All that is like no Dissenters that I have ever known in all my life whatever," replied the Welsh lady somewhat vehemently, with a very distinct intonation of the land. " And have you heard them speak of the bright light that shone at midnight from the church ? "

CHAPTER III

A SECRET IN A SECRET PLACE

NOW here was I altogether at a loss and quite bewildered. The children broke into the conversation of the two ladies and cut it all short, just as the midnight lights from the church came on the field, and when the little girls and boys went back again to the sands whooping, the tide of talk had turned, and Mrs. Harland and Mrs. Williams were quite safe and at home with Janey's measles, and a wonderful treatment for infantile earache, as exemplified in the case of Trevor. There was no more to be got out of them, evidently, so I left the beach, crossed the harbour causeway, and drank beer at the " Fishermen's Rest " till it was time to climb up two miles of deep lane and catch the train for Penvro, where I was staying. And I went up the lane, as I say, in a kind of amazement ; and not so much, I think, because of evidences and hints of things strange to the senses, such as the

savour of incense where no incense had
smoked for three hundred and fifty years
and more, or the story of bright light shining
from the dark, closed church at dead of
night, as because of that sentence of thanksgiving " for paradise in meat and in drink."

For the sun went down and the evening
fell as I climbed the long hill through the
deep woods and the high meadows, and the
scent of all the green things rose from the
earth and from the heart of the wood, and
at a turn of the lane far below was the
misty glimmer of the still sea, and from far
below its deep murmur sounded as it washed
on the little hidden, enclosed bay where
Llantrisant stands. And I thought, if there
be paradise in meat and in drink, so much the
more is there paradise in the scent of the
green leaves at evening and in the appearance of the sea and in the redness of the sky ;
and there came to me a certain vision of a
real world about us all the while, of a
language that was only secret because we
would not take the trouble to listen to it
and discern it.

It was almost dark when I got to the
station, and here were the few feeble oil
lamps lit, glimmering in that lonely land,

where the way is long from farm to farm. The train came on its way, and I got into it; and just as we moved from the station I noticed a group under one of those dim lamps. A woman and her child had got out, and they were being welcomed by a man who had been waiting for them. I had not noticed his face as I stood on the platform, but now I saw it as he pointed down the hill towards Llantrisant, and I think I was almost frightened.

He was a young man, a farmer's son, I would say, dressed in rough brown clothes, and as different from old Mr. Evans, the rector, as one man might be from another. But on his face, as I saw it in the lamplight, there was the like brightening that I had seen on the face of the rector. It was an illuminated face, glowing with an ineffable joy, and I thought it rather gave light to the platform lamp than received light from it. The woman and her child, I inferred, were strangers to the place, and had come to pay a visit to the young man's family. They had looked about them in bewilderment, half alarmed, before they saw him; and then his face was radiant in their sight, and it was easy to see that all their troubles were

ended and over. A wayside station and a
darkening country; and it was as if they
were welcomed by shining, immortal gladness—even into paradise.

   .   .   .   .   .

But though there seemed in a sense light
all about my ways, I was myself still quite
bewildered. I could see, indeed, that something strange had happened or was happening in the little town hidden under the
hill, but there was so far no clue to the
mystery, or rather, the clue had been offered
to me, and I had not taken it, I had not
even known that it was there; since we do
not so much as see what we have determined,
without judging, to be incredible, even
though it be held up before our eyes. The
dialogue that the Welsh Mrs. Williams had
reported to her English friend might have
set me on the right way; but the right way
was outside all my limits of possibility, outside the circle of my thought. The palæ-
ontologist might see monstrous, significant
marks in the slime of a river bank, but he
would never draw the conclusions that his
own peculiar science would seem to suggest
to him; he would choose any explanation

rather than the obvious, since the obvious would also be the outrageous—according to our established habit of thought, which we deem final.

.   .   .   .   .

The next day I took all these strange things with me for consideration to a certain place that I knew of not far from Penvro. I was now in the early stages of the jig-saw process, or rather I had only a few pieces before me, and—to continue the figure—my difficulty was this: that though the markings on each piece seemed to have design and significance, yet I could not make the wildest guess as to the nature of the whole picture, of which these were the parts. I had clearly seen that there was a great secret ; I had seen that on the face of the young farmer on the platform of Llantrisant station ; and in my mind there was all the while the picture of him going down the dark, steep, winding lane that led to the town and the sea, going down through the heart of the wood, with light about him.

But there was bewilderment in the thought of this, and in the endeavour to match it with the perfumed church and the scraps of talk that I had heard and the rumour of midnight brightness; and though Penvro is by no means populous, I thought I would go to a certain solitary place called the Old Camp Head, which looks towards Cornwall and to the great deeps that roll beyond Cornwall to the far ends of the world; a place where fragments of dreams —they seemed such then—might, perhaps, be gathered into the clearness of vision.

It was some years since I had been to the Head, and I had gone on that last time and on a former visit by the cliffs, a rough and difficult path. Now I chose a landward way, which the county map seemed to justify, though doubtfully, as regarded the last part of the journey. So I went inland and climbed the hot summer by-roads, till I came at last to a lane which gradually turned turfy and grass-grown, and then on high ground, ceased to be. It left me at a gate in a hedge of old thorns; and across the field beyond there seemed to be some faint indications of a track. One would judge that sometimes men did pass by that way, but not often.

It was high ground but not within sight

of the sea. But the breath of the sea blew
about the hedge of thorns, and came with
a keen savour to the nostrils. The ground
sloped gently from the gate and then rose
again to a ridge, where a white farmhouse
stood all alone. I passed by this farmhouse,
threading an uncertain way, followed a
hedgerow doubtfully; and saw suddenly
before me the Old Camp, and beyond it the
sapphire plain of waters and the mist where
sea and sky met. Steep from my feet the
hill fell away, a land of gorse-blossom, red-
gold and mellow, of glorious purple heather.
It fell into a hollow that went down,
shining with rich green bracken, to the
glimmering sea; and before me and beyond
the hollow rose a height of turf, bastioned at
the summit with the awful, age-old walls of
the Old Camp; green, rounded circum-
vallations, wall within wall, tremendous,
with their myriad years upon them.

.   .   .   .   .

Within these smoothed, green mounds,
looking across the shining and changing of
the waters in the happy sunlight, I took out
the bread and cheese and beer that I had
carried in a bag, and ate and drank, and lit

my pipe, and set myself to think over the enigmas of Llantrisant. And I had scarcely done so when, a good deal to my annoyance, a man came climbing up over the green ridges, and took up his stand close by, and stared out to sea. He nodded to me, and began with " Fine weather for the harvest " in the approved manner, and so sat down and engaged me in a net of talk. He was of Wales, it seemed, but from a different part of the country, and was staying for a few days with relations—at the white farmhouse which I had passed on my way. His tale of nothing flowed on to his pleasure and my pain, till he fell suddenly on Llantrisant and its doings. I listened then with wonder, and here is his tale condensed. Though it must be clearly understood that the man's evidence was only second-hand; he had heard it from his cousin, the farmer.

So, to be brief, it appeared that there had been a long feud at Llantrisant between a local solicitor, Lewis Prothero (we will say), and a farmer named James. There had been a quarrel about some trifle, which had grown more and more bitter as the two parties forgot the merits of the original dispute, and by some means or other, which

I could not well understand, the lawyer had got the small freeholder " under his thumb." James, I think, had given a bill of sale in a bad season, and Prothero had bought it up; and the end was that the farmer was turned out of the old house, and was lodging in a cottage. People said he would have to take a place on his own farm as a labourer; he went about in dreadful misery, piteous to see. It was thought by some that he might very well murder the lawyer, if he met him.

They did meet, in the middle of the market-place at Llantrisant one Saturday in June. The farmer was a little black man, and he gave a shout of rage, and the people were rushing at him to keep him off Prothero.

" And then," said my informant, " I will tell you what happened. This lawyer, as they tell me, he is a great big brawny fellow, with a big jaw and a wide mouth, and a red face and red whiskers. And there he was in his black coat and his high hard hat, and all his money at his back, as you may say. And, indeed, he did fall down on his knees in the dust there in the street in front of Philip James, and every one could see that terror was upon him. And he did beg Philip James's pardon, and beg of him to have mercy, and he did implore him by God and man and the saints of paradise. And my cousin, John Jenkins, Penmawr, he do tell me that the tears were falling from Lewis Prothero's eyes like the rain. And he put his hand into his pocket and drew out the deed of Pantyreos, Philip James's old farm that was, and did give him the farm back and a hundred pounds for the stock that was on it, and two hundred pounds, all in notes of the bank, for amendment and consolation.

"And then, from what they do tell me, all the people did go mad, crying and weeping and calling out all manner of things at the top of their voices. And at last nothing would do but they must all go up to the churchyard, and there Philip James and Lewis Prothero they swear friendship to one another for a long age before the old cross, and everyone sings praises. And my cousin he do declare to me that there were men standing in that crowd that he did never see before in Llantrisant in all his life, and his heart was shaken within him as if it had been in a whirlwind."

I had listened to all this in silence. I said then:

"What does your cousin mean by that ?

Men that he had never seen in Llantrisant ?
What men ? ''

'' The people,'' he said very slowly, '' call
them the Fishermen.''

And suddenly there came into my mind
the '' Rich Fisherman '' who in the old
legend guards the holy mystery of the
Graal.

CHAPTER IV

THE RINGING OF THE BELL

SO far I have not told the story of the things of Llantrisant, but rather the story of how I stumbled upon them and among them, perplexed and wholly astray, seeking, but yet not knowing at all what I sought; bewildered now and again by circumstances which seemed to me wholly inexplicable; devoid, not so much of the key to the enigma, but of the key to the nature of the enigma. You cannot begin to solve a puzzle till you know what the puzzle is about. " Yards divided by minutes," said the mathematical master to me long ago, " will give neither pigs, sheep, nor oxen." He was right; though his manner on this and on all other occasions was highly offensive. This is enough of the personal process, as I may call it; and here follows the story of what happened at Llantrisant last summer, the story as I pieced it together at last.

The Ringing of the Bell

It all began, it appears, on a hot day, early in last June ; so far as I can make out, on the first Saturday in the month. There was a deaf old woman, a Mrs. Parry, who lived by herself in a lonely cottage a mile or so from the town. She came into the market-place early on the Saturday morning in a state of some excitement, and as soon as she had taken up her usual place on the pavement by the churchyard, with her ducks and eggs and a few very early potatoes, she began to tell her neighbours about her having heard the sound of a great bell. The good women on each side smiled at one another behind Mrs. Parry's back, for one had to bawl into her ear before she could make out what one meant ; and Mrs. Williams, Penycoed, bent over and yelled : " What bell should that be, Mrs. Parry ? There's no church near you up at Penrhiw. Do you hear what nonsense she talks ? " said Mrs. Williams in a low voice to Mrs. Morgan. " As if she could hear any bell, whatever."

" What makes you talk nonsense yourself ? " said Mrs. Parry, to the amazement of the two women. " I can hear a bell as well as you, Mrs. Williams, and as well as your whispers either."

And there is the fact, which is not to be disputed; though the deductions from it may be open to endless disputations; this old woman who had been all but stone deaf for twenty years—the defect had always been in her family—could suddenly hear on this June morning as well as anybody else. And her two old friends stared at her, and it was some time before they had appeased her indignation, and induced her to talk about the bell.

It had happened in the early morning, which was very misty. She had been gathering sage in her garden, high on a round hill looking over the sea. And there came in her ears a sort of throbbing and singing and trembling, " as if there were music coming out of the earth," and then something seemed to break in her head, and all the birds began to sing and make melody together, and the leaves of the poplars round the garden fluttered in the breeze that rose from the sea, and the cock crowed far off at Twyn, and the dog barked down in Kemeys Valley. But above all these sounds, unheard for so many years, there thrilled the deep and chanting note of the bell, " like a bell and a man's voice singing at once."

They stared again at her and at one another. " Where did it sound from ? " asked one. " It came sailing across the sea," answered Mrs. Parry quite composedly, " and I did hear it coming nearer and nearer to the land."

" Well, indeed," said Mrs. Morgan, " it was a ship's bell then, though I can't make out why they would be ringing like that."

" It was not ringing on any ship, Mrs. Morgan," said Mrs. Parry.

" Then where do you think it was ringing ? "

" Ym Mharadwys," replied Mrs. Parry. Now that means " in Paradise," and the two others changed the conversation quickly. They thought that Mrs. Parry had got back her hearing suddenly—such things did happen now and then—and that the shock had made her " a bit queer." And this explanation would no doubt have stood its ground, if it had not been for other experiences. Indeed, the local doctor who had treated Mrs. Parry for a dozen years, not for her deafness, which he took to be hopeless and beyond cure, but for a tiresome and recurrent winter cough, sent an account of the case to a colleague at Bristol, suppressing, naturally enough, the reference to Paradise. The Bristol physician gave it as his opinion that the symptoms were absolutely what might have been expected. "You have here, in all probability," he wrote, "the sudden breaking down of an old obstruction in the aural passage, and I should quite expect this process to be accompanied by tinnitus of a pronounced and even violent character."

.   .   .   .   .

But for the other experiences ? As the morning wore on and drew to noon, high market, and to the utmost brightness of that summer day, all the stalls and the streets were full of rumours and of awed faces. Now from one lonely farm, now from another, men and women came and told the story of how they had listened in the early morning with thrilling hearts to the thrilling music of a bell that was like no bell ever heard before. And it seemed that many people in the town had been roused, they knew not how, from sleep ; waking up, as one of them said, as if bells were ringing and the organ playing, and a choir of sweet voices singing all together : " There were such melodies and songs that my heart was full of joy."

And a little past noon some fishermen who had been out all night returned, and brought a wonderful story into the town of what they had heard in the mist ; and one of them said he had seen something go by at a little distance from his boat. " It was all golden and bright," he said, " and there was glory about it." Another fisherman declared " there was a song upon the water that was like heaven."

And here I would say in parenthesis that on returning to town I sought out a very old friend of mine, a man who has devoted a lifetime to strange and esoteric studies. I thought that I had a tale that would interest him profoundly, but I found that he heard me with a good deal of indifference. And at this very point of the sailors' stories I remember saying : " Now what do you make of that ? Don't you think it's extremely curious ? " He replied : " I hardly think so. Possibly the sailors were lying ; possibly it happened as they say. Well ; that sort of thing has always been happening." I give my friend's opinion ; I make no comment on it.

Let it be noted that there was something remarkable as to the manner in which the sound of the bell was heard—or supposed to be heard. There are, no doubt, mysteries in sound as in all else ; indeed, I am informed that during one of the horrible outrages that have been perpetrated on London during this autumn there was an instance of a great block of workmen's dwellings in which the only person who heard the crash of a particular bomb falling was an old deaf woman, who had been fast asleep till the moment of the explosion. This is strange enough of a sound that was entirely in the natural (and horrible) order ; and so it was at Llantrisant, where the sound was either a collective auditory hallucination or a manifestation of what is conveniently, if inaccurately, called the supernatural order.

For the thrill of the bell did not reach to all ears—or hearts. Deaf Mrs. Parry heard it in her lonely cottage garden, high above the misty sea ; but then, in a farm on the other or western side of Llantrisant, a little child, scarcely three years old, was the only one out of a household of ten people who heard anything. He called out in stammering baby Welsh something that sounded like

The Ringing of the Bell

" Clychau fawr, clychau fawr "—the great
bells, the great bells—and his mother won-
dered what he was talking about. Of the
crews of half a dozen trawlers that were
swinging from side to side in the mist, not
more than four men had any tale to tell.
And so it was that for an hour or two the
man who had heard nothing suspected his
neighbour who had heard marvels of lying ;
and it was some time before the mass of
evidence coming from all manner of diverse
and remote quarters convinced the people
that there was a true story here. A might
suspect B, his neighbour, of making up a
tale ; but when C, from some place on the
hills five miles away, and D, the fisherman on
the waters, each had a like report, then it
was clear that something had happened.

.   .   .   .   .

And even then, as they told me, the signs
to be seen upon the people were stranger
than the tales told by them and among them.
It has struck me that many people in reading
some of the phrases that I have reported will
dismiss them with laughter as very poor and
fantastic inventions ; fishermen, they will
say, do not speak of " a song like heaven " or

of " a glory about it." And I dare say this would be a just enough criticism if I were reporting English fishermen; but, odd though it may be, Wales has not yet lost the last shreds of the grand manner. And let it be remembered also that in most cases such phrases are translated from another language, that is, from the Welsh.

So, they come trailing, let us say, fragments of the cloud of glory in their common speech; and so, on this Saturday, they began to display, uneasily enough in many cases, their consciousness that the things that were reported were of their ancient right and former custom. The comparison is not quite fair; but conceive Hardy's old Durbeyfield suddenly waking from long slumber to find himself in a noble thirteenth-century hall, waited on by kneeling pages, smiled on by sweet ladies in silken côtehardies.

So by evening time there had come to the old people the recollection of stories that their fathers had told them as they sat round the hearth of winter nights, fifty, sixty, seventy years ago; stories of the wonderful bell of Teilo Sant, that had sailed across the glassy seas from Syon, that was called a portion of Paradise, " and the sound of its ringing was like the perpetual choir of the angels."

Such things were remembered by the old and told to the young that evening, in the streets of the town and in the deep lanes that climbed far hills. The sun went down to the mountain red with fire like a burnt offering, the sky turned violet, the sea was purple, as one told another of the wonder that had returned to the land after long ages.

CHAPTER V

THE ROSE OF FIRE

IT was during the next nine days, counting from that Saturday early in June—the first Saturday in June, as I believe—that Llantrisant and all the regions about became possessed either by an extraordinary set of hallucinations or by a visitation of great marvels.

This is not the place to strike the balance between the two possibilities. The evidence is, no doubt, readily available ; the matter is open to systematic investigation.

But this may be said : The ordinary man, in the ordinary passages of his life, accepts in the main the evidence of his senses, and is entirely right in doing so. He says that he sees a cow, that he sees a stone wall, and that the cow and the stone wall are " there." This is very well for all the practical purposes of life, but I believe that the metaphysicians are by no means so easily satisfied as to the reality of the stone wall and the cow. Perhaps they might allow that both objects are " there " in the sense that one's reflection is in a glass ; there is an actuality, but is there a reality external to oneself ? In any event, it is solidly agreed that, supposing a real existence, this much is certain—it is not in the least like our conception of it. The ant and the microscope will quickly convince us that we do not see things as they really are, even supposing that we see them at all. If we could " see " the real cow she would appear utterly incredible, as incredible as the things I am to relate.

Now, there is nothing that I know much more unconvincing than the stories of the red light on the sea. Several sailors, men on small coasting ships, who were working up or down the Channel on that Saturday night, spoke of " seeing " the red light, and it must be said that there is a very tolerable agreement in their tales. All make the time as between midnight of the Saturday and one o'clock on the Sunday morning. Two of those sailormen are precise as to the time of the apparition ; they fix it by elaborate calculations of their own as occurring at 12.20 a.m. And the story ?

A red light, a burning spark seen far away

in the darkness, taken at the first moment of seeing for a signal, and probably an enemy signal. Then it approached at a tremendous speed, and one man said he took it to be the port light of some new kind of navy motor-boat which was developing a rate hitherto unheard of, a hundred or a hundred and fifty knots an hour. And then, in the third instant of the sight, it was clear that this was no earthly speed. At first a red spark in the farthest distance ; then a rushing lamp ; and then, as if in an incredible point of time, it swelled into a vast rose of fire that filled all the sea and all the sky and hid the stars and possessed the land. " I thought the end of the world had come," one of the sailors said.

And then, an instant more, and it was gone from them, and four of them say that there was a red spark on Chapel Head, where the old grey chapel of St. Teilo stands, high above the water, in a cleft of the lime-stone rocks.

And thus the sailors ; and thus their tales are incredible ; but *they* are not incredible. I believe that men of the highest eminence in physical science have testified to the occurrence of phenomena every whit as marvellous, to things as absolutely opposed to all natural order, as we conceive it ; and it may be said that nobody minds them. "That sort of thing has always been happening," as my friend remarked to me. But the men, whether or no the fire had ever been without them, there was no doubt that it was now within them, for it burned in their eyes. They were purged as if they had passed through the Furnace of the Sages, governed with Wisdom that the alchemists know. They spoke without much difficulty of what they had seen, or had seemed to see, with their eyes, but hardly at all of what their hearts had known when for a moment the glory of the fiery rose had been about them.

For some weeks afterwards they were still, as it were, amazed ; almost, I would say, incredulous. If there had been nothing more than the splendid and fiery appearance, showing and vanishing, I do believe that they themselves would have discredited their own senses and denied the truth of their own tales. And one does not dare to say whether they would not have been right. Men like Sir William Crookes and Sir Oliver Lodge are certainly to be heard with respect, and they bear witness to all manner of apparent eversions of laws which we, or most of us, consider far more deeply founded than the ancient hills. They may be justified; but in our hearts we doubt. We cannot wholly believe in inner sincerity that the solid table did rise, without mechanical reason or cause, into the air, and so defy that which we name the " law of gravitation." I know what may be said on the other side; I know that there is no true question of " law " in the case; that the law of gravitation really means just this: that I have never seen a table rising without mechanical aid, or an apple, detached from the bough, soaring to the skies instead of falling to the ground. The so-called law is just the sum of common observation and nothing more; yet I say, in our hearts we do not believe that the tables rise; much less do we believe in the rose of fire that for a moment swallowed up the skies and seas and shores of the Welsh coast last June.

And the men who saw it would have invented fairy tales to account for it, I say again, if it had not been for that which was within them.

They said, all of them, and it was certain now that they spoke the truth, that in the moment of the vision, every pain and ache and malady in their bodies had passed away. One man had been vilely drunk on venomous spirit, procured at " Jobson's Hole " down by the Cardiff Docks. He was horribly ill ; he had crawled up from his bunk for a little fresh air ; and in an instant his horrors and his deadly nausea had left him. Another man was almost desperate with the raging hammering pain of an abscess on a tooth ; he says that when the red flame came near he felt as if a dull, heavy blow had fallen on his jaw, and then the pain was quite gone ; he could scarcely believe that there had been any pain there.

And they all bear witness to an extra-ordinary exaltation of the senses. It is indescribable, this ; for they cannot describe it. They are amazed, again ; they do not in the least profess to know what happened ; but there is no more possibility of shaking their evidence than there is a possibility of shaking the evidence of a man who says that water is wet and fire hot.

" I felt a bit queer afterwards," said one of them, " and I steadied myself by the mast, and I can't tell how I felt as I touched it. I didn't know that touching a thing like a mast could be better than a big drink when you're thirsty, or a soft pillow when you're sleepy."

I heard other instances of this state of things, as I must vaguely call it, since I do not know what else to call it. But I suppose we can all agree that to the man in average health, the average impact of the external world on his senses is a matter of indifference. The average impact; a harsh scream, the bursting of a motor tyre, any violent assault on the aural nerves will annoy him, and he may say " damn." Then, on the other hand, the man who is not " fit " will easily be annoyed and irritated by someone pushing past him in a crowd, by the ringing of a bell, by the sharp closing of a book.

But so far as I could judge from the talk of these sailors, the average impact of the external world had become to them a fountain of pleasure. Their nerves were on edge, but an edge to receive exquisite sensuous impressions. The touch of the rough mast, for example; that was a joy far greater than is the joy of fine silk to some luxurious skins; they drank water and stared as if they had been *fins gourmets* tasting an amazing wine; the creak and whine of their ship on its slow way were as exquisite as the rhythm and song of a Bach fugue to an amateur of music.

And then, within; these rough fellows have their quarrels and strifes and variances and envyings like the rest of us; but that was all over between them that had seen the rosy light; old enemies shook hands heartily, and roared with laughter as they confessed one to another what fools they had been.

" I can't exactly say how it has happened or what has happened at all," said one, " but if you have all the world and the glory of it, how can you fight for fivepence ? "

.   .   .   .   .

The church of Llantrisant is a typical example of a Welsh parish church, before the evil and horrible period of " restoration."

This lower world is a palace of lies, and of all foolish lies there is none more insane than a certain vague fable about the mediæval freemasons, a fable which somehow imposed itself upon the cold intellect of Hallam the historian. The story is, in brief, that throughout the Gothic period, at any rate, the art and craft of church building were executed by wandering guilds of " free-

masons," possessed of various secrets of
building and adornment, which they employed wherever they went. If this nonsense were true, the Gothic of Cologne
would be as the Gothic of Colne, and the
Gothic of Arles like to the Gothic of Abing-
don. It is so grotesquely untrue that almost
every county, let alone every country, has
its distinctive style in Gothic architecture.
Arfon is in the west of Wales ; its churches
have marks and features which distinguish
them from the churches in the east of Wales.

The Llantrisant church has that primitive
division between nave and chancel which
only very foolish people decline to recognise
as equivalent to the Oriental iconostasis and
as the origin of the Western rood-screen. A
solid wall divided the church into two por-
tions ; in the centre was a narrow opening
with a rounded arch, through which those
who sat towards the middle of the church
could see the small, red-carpeted altar and
the three roughly shaped lancet windows
above it.

The " reading pew " was on the outer side
of this wall of partition, and here the rector
did his service, the choir being grouped in
seats about him. On the inner side were the

pews of certain privileged houses of the town and district.

On the Sunday morning the people were all in their accustomed places, not without a certain exultation in their eyes, not without a certain expectation of they knew not what. The bells stopped ringing, the rector, in his old-fashioned, ample surplice, entered the reading-desk, and gave out the hymn: "My God, and is Thy Table spread."

And, as the singing began, all the people who were in the pews within the wall came out of them and streamed through the archway into the nave. They took what places they could find up and down the church, and the rest of the congregation looked at them in amazement.

Nobody knew what had happened. Those whose seats were next to the aisle tried to peer into the chancel, to see what had happened or what was going on there. But somehow the light flamed so brightly from the windows above the altar, those being the only windows in the chancel, one small lancet in the south wall excepted, that no one could see anything at all.

" It was as if a veil of gold adorned with jewels was hanging there," one man said ;

and indeed there are a few odds and scraps of old painted glass left in the eastern lancets.

But there were few in the church who did not hear now and again voices speaking beyond the veil.

CHAPTER VI

OLWEN'S DREAM

THE well-to-do and dignified personages who left their pews in the chancel of Llantrisant Church and came hurrying into the nave could give no explanation of what they had done. They felt, they said, that they "had to go," and to go quickly; they were driven out, as it were, by a secret, irresistible command. But all who were present in the church that morning were amazed, though all exulted in their hearts; for they, like the sailors who saw the rose of fire on the waters, were filled with a joy that was literally ineffable, since they could not utter it or interpret it to themselves.

And they too, like the sailors, were transmuted, or the world was transmuted for them. They experienced what the doctors call a sense of *bien être*, but a *bien être* raised to the highest power. Old men felt young again, eyes that had been growing dim now saw clearly, and saw a world that was like

Paradise, the same world, it is true, but a world rectified and glowing, as if an inner flame shone in all things, and behind all things.

And the difficulty in recording this state is this, that it is so rare an experience that no set language to express it is in existence. A shadow of its raptures and ecstasies is found in the highest poetry; there are phrases in ancient books telling of the Celtic saints that dimly hint at it; some of the old Italian masters of painting had known it, for the light of it shines in their skies and about the battlements of their cities that are founded on magic hills. But these are but broken hints.

It is not poetic to go to Apothecaries' Hall for similes. But for many years I kept by me an article from the *Lancet* or the *British Medical Journal*—I forget which—in which a doctor gave an account of certain experiments he had conducted with a drug called the Mescal Button, or Anhelonium Lewinii. He said that while under the influence of the drug he had but to shut his eyes, and immediately before him there would rise incredible Gothic cathedrals, of such majesty and splendour and glory that no heart had ever conceived. They seemed to surge from the depths to the very heights of heaven, their spires swayed amongst the clouds and the stars, they were fretted with admirable imagery. And as he gazed, he would presently become aware that all the stones were living stones, that they were quickening and palpitating, and then that they were glowing jewels, say, emeralds, sapphires, rubies, opals, but of hues that the mortal eye had never seen.

That description gives, I think, some faint notion of the nature of the transmuted world into which these people by the sea had entered, a world quickened and glorified and full of pleasures. Joy and wonder were on all faces; but the deepest joy and the greatest wonder were on the face of the rector. For he had heard through the veil the Greek word for " holy," three times repeated. And he, who had once been a horrified assistant at High Mass in a foreign church, recognised the perfume of incense that filled the place from end to end.

.   .   .   .   .

It was on that Sunday night that Olwen Phillips of Croeswen dreamed her wonderful dream. She was a girl of sixteen, the daughter of small farming people, and for many months she had been doomed to certain death. Consumption, which flourishes in that damp, warm climate, had laid hold of her; not only her lungs but her whole system was a mass of tuberculosis. As is common enough, she had enjoyed many fallacious brief recoveries in the early stages of the disease, but all hope had long been over, and now for the last few weeks she had seemed to rush vehemently to death. The doctor had come on the Saturday morning, bringing with him a colleague. They had both agreed that the girl's case was in its last stages. " She cannot possibly last more than a day or two," said the local doctor to her mother. He came again on the Sunday morning and found his patient perceptibly worse, and soon afterwards she sank into a heavy sleep, and her mother thought that she would never wake from it.

The girl slept in an inner room communicating with the room occupied by her father and mother. The door between was kept open, so that Mrs. Phillips could hear her daughter if she called to her in the night. And Olwen called to her mother that night,

just as the dawn was breaking. It was no
faint summons from a dying bed that came
to the mother's ears, but a loud cry that rang
through the house, a cry of great gladness.
Mrs. Phillips started up from sleep in wild
amazement, wondering what could have
happened. And then she saw Olwen, who
had not been able to rise from her bed for
many weeks past, standing in the doorway
in the faint light of the growing day. The
girl called to her mother: "Mam! mam!
It is all over. I am quite well again."

Mrs. Phillips roused her husband, and
they sat up in bed staring, not knowing on
earth, as they said afterwards, what had
been done with the world. Here was their
poor girl wasted to a shadow, lying on her
death-bed, and the life sighing from her with
every breath, and her voice, when she last
uttered it, so weak that one had to put one's
ear to her mouth. And here in a few hours
she stood up before them ; and even in that
faint light they could see that she was
changed almost beyond knowing. And,
indeed, Mrs. Phillips said that for a moment
or two she fancied that the Germans must
have come and killed them in their sleep, and
so they were all dead together. But Olwen

called out again, so the mother lit a candle and got up and went tottering across the room, and there was Olwen all gay and plump again, smiling with shining eyes. Her mother led her into her own room, and set down the candle there, and felt her daughter's flesh, and burst into prayers and tears of wonder and delight, and thanksgivings, and held the girl again to be sure that she was not deceived. And then Olwen told her dream, though she thought it was not a dream.

She said she woke up in the deep darkness, and she knew the life was fast going from her. She could not move so much as a finger, she tried to cry out, but no sound came from her lips. She felt that in another instant the whole world would fall from her—her heart was full of agony. And as the last breath was passing her lips, she heard a very faint, sweet sound, like the tinkling of a silver bell. It came from far away, from over by Ty-newydd. She forgot her agony and listened, and even then, she says, she felt the swirl of the world as it came back to her. And the sound of the bell swelled and grew louder, and it thrilled all through her body, and the life was in it. And as the bell rang and trembled in her ears, a faint light touched the wall of her room and reddened, till the whole room was full of rosy fire. And then she saw standing before her bed three men in blood-coloured robes with shining faces. And one man held a golden bell in his hand. And the second man held up something shaped like the top of a table. It was like a great jewel, and it was of a blue colour, and there were rivers of silver and of gold running through it and flowing as quick streams flow, and there were pools in it as if violets had been poured out into water, and then it was green as the sea near the shore, and then it was the sky at night with all the stars shining, and then the sun and the moon came down and washed in it. And the third man held up high above this a cup that was like a rose on fire ; " there was a great burning in it, and a dropping of blood in it, and a red cloud above it, and I saw a great secret. And I heard a voice that sang nine times, ' Glory and praise to the Conqueror of Death, to the Fountain of Life immortal.' Then the red light went from the wall, and it was all darkness, and the bell rang faint again by Capel Teilo, and then I got up and called to you."

The doctor came on the Monday morning with the death certificate in his pocket-book, and Olwen ran out to meet him. I have quoted his phrase in the first chapter of this record: "A kind of resurrection of the body." He made a most careful examination of the girl; he has stated that he found that every trace of disease had disappeared. He left on the Sunday morning a patient entering into the coma that precedes death, a body condemned utterly and ready for the grave. He met at the garden gate on the Monday morning a young woman in whom life sprang up like a fountain, in whose body life laughed and rejoiced as if it had been a river flowing from an unending well.

.   .   .   .   .

Now this is the place to ask one of those questions—there are many such—which cannot be answered. The question is as to the continuance of tradition; more especially as to the continuance of tradition among the Welsh Celts of to-day. On the one hand, such waves and storms have gone over them. The wave of the heathen Saxons went over them, then the wave of Latin mediævalism, then the waters of Anglicanism; last of all

the flood of their queer Calvinistic Method-
ism, half Puritan, half pagan. It may well be
asked whether any memory can possibly have
survived such a series of deluges. I have said
that the old people of Llantrisant had their
tales of the Bell of Teilo Sant ; but these
were but vague and broken recollections.
And then there is the name by which the
" strangers " who were seen in the market-
place were known ; that is more precise.
Students of the Graal legend know that the
keeper of the Graal in the romances is the
" King Fisherman," or the " Rich Fisherman " ; students of Celtic hagiology know
that it was prophesied before the birth of
Dewi (or David) that he should be " a man
of aquatic life," that another legend tells
how a little child, destined to be a saint,
was discovered on a stone in the river, how
through his childhood a fish for his nourish-
ment was found on that stone every day,
while another saint, Ilar, if I remember,
was expressly known as " The Fisherman."
But has the memory of all this persisted in
the church-going and chapel-going people
of Wales at the present day ? It is difficult
to say. There is the affair of the Healing
Cup of Nant Eos, or Tregaron Healing Cup,

as it is also called. It is only a few years ago since it was shown to a wandering harper, who treated it lightly, and then spent a wretched night, as he said, and came back penitently and was left alone with the sacred vessel to pray over it, till " his mind was at rest." That was in 1887.

Then for my part—I only know modern Wales on the surface, I am sorry to say—I remember three or four years ago speaking to my temporary landlord of certain relics of Saint Teilo, which are supposed to be in the keeping of a particular family in that country. The landlord is a very jovial, merry fellow, and I observed with some astonishment that his ordinary, easy manner was completely altered as he said, gravely, " That will be over there, up by the mountain," pointing vaguely to the north. And he changed the subject, as a Freemason changes the subject.

There the matter lies, and its appositeness to the story of Llantrisant is this : that the dream of Olwen Phillips was, in fact, the Vision of the Holy Graal.

CHAPTER VII

THE MASS OF THE SANGRAAL

"*FFEIRIADWYR Melcisidec! Ffeir-iadwyr Melcisidec!*" shouted the old Calvinistic Methodist deacon with the grey beard. "Priesthood of Melchizedek! Priesthood of Melchizedek!"

And he went on:

"The Bell that is like *y glwys yr angel ym mharadwys*—the joy of the angels in Paradise—is returned; the Altar that is of a colour that no men can discern is returned, the Cup that came from Syon is returned, the ancient Offering is restored, the Three Saints have come back to the church of the *tri sant*, the Three Holy Fishermen are amongst us, and their net is full. *Gogoniant, gogoniant*—glory, glory!"

Then another Methodist began to recite in Welsh a verse from Wesley's hymn.

God still respects Thy sacrifice,
Its savour sweet doth always please;
The Offering smokes through earth and skies,
Diffusing life and joy and peace;

To these Thy lower courts it comes
And fills them with Divine perfumes.

The whole church was full, as the old
books tell, of the odour of the rarest
spiceries. There were lights shining within
the sanctuary, through the narrow archway.
This was the beginning of the end of
what befell at Llantrisant. For it was the
Sunday after that night on which Olwen
Phillips had been restored from death to life.
There was not a single chapel of the Dissenters open in the town that day. The
Methodists with their minister and their
deacons and all the Nonconformists had
returned on this Sunday morning to " the
old hive." One would have said, a church
of the Middle Ages, a church in Ireland to-
day. Every seat—save those in the chancel
—was full, all the aisles were full, the
churchyard was full; everyone on his
knees, and the old rector kneeling before
the door into the holy place.

Yet they can say but very little of what
was done beyond the veil. There was no
attempt to perform the usual service; when
the bells had stopped the old deacon raised
his cry, and priest and people fell down on

72

their knees as they thought they heard a choir within singing " Alleluya, alleluya, alleluya." And as the bells in the tower ceased ringing, there sounded the thrill of the bell from Syon, and the golden veil of sunlight fell across the door into the altar, and the heavenly voices began their melodies.

A voice like a trumpet cried from within the brightness :

Agyos, Agyos, Agyos.

And the people, as if an age-old memory stirred in them, replied :

Agyos yr Tâd, agyos yr Mab, agyos yr Yspryd Glan. Sant, sant, sant, Drindod sant vendigeid. Sanctus Arglwydd Dduw Sabaoth, Dominus Deus.

There was a voice that cried and sang from within the altar ; most of the people had heard some faint echo of it in the chapels ; a voice rising and falling and soaring in awful modulations that rang like the trumpet of the Last Angel. The people beat upon their breasts, the tears were like rain of the mountains on their cheeks ; those that were able fell down flat on their faces before the glory of the veil. They said afterwards that men of the hills, twenty miles away, heard that cry and that singing, roaring upon them on the wind, and they fell down on their faces, and cried, " The offering is accomplished," knowing nothing of what they said.

There were a few who saw three come out of the door of the sanctuary, and stand for a moment on the pace before the door. These three were in dyed vesture, red as blood. One stood before two, looking to the west, and he rang the bell. And they say that all the birds of the wood, and all the waters of the sea, and all the leaves of the trees, and all the winds of the high rocks uttered their voices with the ringing of the bell. And the second and the third; they turned their faces one to another. The second held up the lost altar that they once called *Sapphirus*, which was like the changing of the sea and of the sky, and like the immixture of gold and silver. And the third heaved up high over the altar a cup that was red with burning and the blood of the offering.

And the old rector cried aloud then before the entrance:

Bendigeid yr Offeren yn oes oesoedd— blessed be the Offering unto the age of ages.

And then the Mass of the Sangraal was

ended, and then began the passing out of
that land of the holy persons and holy
things that had returned to it after the
long years. It seemed, indeed, to many
that the thrilling sound of the bell was in
their ears for days, even for weeks after
that Sunday morning. But thenceforth
neither bell nor altar nor cup was seen by
anyone ; not openly, that is, but only in
dreams by day and by night. Nor did the
people see Strangers again in the market of
Llantrisant, nor in the lonely places where
certain persons oppressed by great affliction
and sorrow had once or twice encountered
them.

    .   .   .   .   .

But that time of visitation will never be
forgotten by the people. Many things happened in the nine days that have not been
set down in this record—or legend. Some
of them were trifling matters, though
strange enough in other times. Thus a man
in the town who had a fierce dog that was
always kept chained up found one day that
the beast had become mild and gentle.

And this is odder : Edward Davies, of
Lanafon, a farmer, was roused from sleep

one night by a queer yelping and barking in his yard. He looked out of the window and saw his sheep-dog playing with a big fox; they were chasing each other by turns, rolling over and over one another, " cutting such capers as I did never see the like," as the astonished farmer put it. And some of the people said that during this season of wonder the corn shot up, and the grass thickened, and the fruit was multiplied on the trees in a very marvellous manner.

More important, it seemed, was the case of Williams, the grocer; though this may have been a purely natural deliverance. Mr. Williams was to marry his daughter Mary to a smart young fellow from Carmarthen, and he was in great distress over it. Not over the marriage itself, but because things had been going very badly with him for some time, and he could not see his way to giving anything like the wedding entertainment that would be expected of him. The wedding was to be on the Saturday—that was the day on which the lawyer, Lewis Prothero, and the farmer, Philip James, were reconciled— and this John Williams, without money or credit, could not think how shame would not be on him for the meagreness and

poverty of the wedding feast. And then on
the Tuesday came a letter from his brother,
David Williams, Australia, from whom he
had not heard for fifteen years. And David,
it seemed, had been making a great deal of
money, and was a bachelor, and here was
with his letter a paper good for a thousand
pounds: "You may as well enjoy it now as
wait till I am dead." This was enough, indeed, one might say; but hardly an hour
after the letter had come the lady from the
big house (Plas Mawr) drove up in all her
grandeur, and went into the shop and said,
"Mr. Williams, your daughter Mary has
always been a very good girl, and my husband and I feel that we must give her some
little thing on her wedding, and we hope
she'll be very happy." It was a gold watch
worth fifteen pounds. And after Lady
Watcyn, advances the old doctor with a
dozen of port, forty years upon it, and a long
sermon on how to decant it. And the old
rector's old wife brings to the beautiful dark
girl two yards of creamy lace, like an en-
chantment, for her wedding veil, and tells
Mary how she wore it for her own wedding
fifty years ago; and the squire, Sir Watcyn,
as if his wife had not been already with a

fine gift, calls from his horse, and brings out
Williams and barks like a dog at him, " Goin'
to have a weddin', eh, Williams ? Can't
have a weddin' without champagne, y'
know ; wouldn't be legal, don't y' know.
So look out for a couple of cases." So
Williams tells the story of the gifts; and
certainly there was never so famous a
wedding in Llantrisant before.

All this, of course, may have been altogether in the natural order ; the " glow," as
they call it, seems more difficult to explain.
For they say that all through the nine days,
and indeed after the time had ended, there
never was a man weary or sick at heart in
Llantrisant, or in the country round it. For
if a man felt that his work of the body or
the mind was going to be too much for his
strength, then there would come to him
of a sudden a warm glow and a thrilling all
over him, and he felt as strong as a giant,
and happier than he had ever been in his
life before, so that lawyer and hedger
each rejoiced in the task that was before
him, as if it were sport and play.

And much more wonderful than this or
any other wonders was forgiveness, with love
to follow it. There were meetings of old

enemies in the market-place and in the street that made the people lift up their hands and declare that it was as if one walked the miraculous streets of Syon.

.   .   .   .   .

But as to the " phenomena," the occurrences for which, in ordinary talk, we should reserve the word " miraculous " ?   Well, what do we know ?   The question that I have already stated comes up again, as to the possible survival of old tradition in a kind of dormant, or torpid, semi-conscious state. In other words, did the people " see " and " hear " what they expected to see and hear ?   This point, or one similar to it, occurred in a debate between Andrew Lang and Anatole France as to the visions of Joan of Arc.   M. France stated that when Joan saw St. Michael, she saw the traditional archangel of the religious art of her day, but to the best of my belief Andrew Lang proved that the visionary figure Joan described was not in the least like the fifteenth-century conception of St. Michael.   So, in the case of Llantrisant, I have stated that there was a sort of tradition about the Holy Bell of Teilo Sant ;   and it is, of course, barely possible that some vague notion of the Graal Cup may have reached even Welsh country folks through Tennyson's "Idylls." But so far I see no reason to suppose that these people had ever heard of the portable altar (called Sapphirus in William of Malmesbury) or of its changing colours "that no man could discern."

And then there are the other questions of the distinction between hallucination and vision, of the average duration of one and the other, and of the possibility of collective hallucination. If a number of people all see (or think they see) the same appearances, can this be merely hallucination? I believe there is a leading case on the matter, which concerns a number of people seeing the same appearance on a church wall in Ireland; but there is, of course, this difficulty, that one may be hallucinated and communicate his impression to the others, telepathically.

But at the last, what do we know?

CPSIA information can be obtained
at www.ICGtesting.com
Printed in the USA
LVHW091940161121
703474LV00003B/136

9 781621 387732